6 - 03

CR

D0466590

For my sister Alexandra, what a woman!
and
My dog, Oliver Wink, what a Pug!

Thanks to Cecilia, Nancy and Andrea
for making this book possible.
Big Joy to Michele Morgan, my seer and muse,
and to Lee Donais
for being my teacher and friend.

Copyright © 2003 by Woodleigh Marx Hubbard

All rights reserved. This book, or parts thereof, may not be reproduced in any form
without permission in writing from the publisher, G. P. Putnam's Sons, a division of
Penguin Putnam Books for Young Readers, 345 Hudson Street, New York, NY 10014.
G. P. Putnam's Sons, Reg. U.S. Pat. & Tm. Off. Published simultaneously in Canada.
Manufactured in China by South China Printing Co. Ltd.
Book designed by Cecilia Yung and Gunta Alexander. Text set in August.
The art was done in pastel watercolor pencils and gouache paint.
Library of Congress Cataloging-in-Publication Data
Hubbard, Woodleigh.
For the love of a pug / Woodleigh Marx Hubbard.
p. cm. Summary: Pictures, easy text, and variations on classic rhymes
celebrate the many sides of the pug dog. [1. Pug—Fiction. 2. Dogs—Fiction.] I. Title.
PZ7.H8624 Fo 2003 [E]—dc21 2002013349 ISBN 0-399-23781-X
1 3 5 7 9 10 8 6 4 2
First Impression

For the Love of a Pug

Woodleigh Marx Hubbard

G. P. Putnam's Sons ♭ New York

There was a Pug who had a curl
Right in the middle of his tail:
When he was good, he was very, very good,
And when he was BAD, he was HORRID.

Good Pug

Naughty Pug

Old Mother Hubbard went to the cupboard
to get her poor Pug a bone.
But when she got there,
the cupboard was bare,
and so the poor Pug had none.

Grumpy Pug

Hangdog Pug

Oh where, oh where has my little Pug gone?
Oh where, oh where can he be?
With his ears so soft and his tail so sweet,

Oh where, oh where can he be?

Digging Pug

Hiding Pug

I see the Pug,
And the Pug sees me;

God bless the Pug,
And God bless me.

Frisky Pug

How much pie could a Pug put away
If a Pug could put away pie?
He'd put away as much pie as a Pug could,
If a Pug could put away pie.

Sloppy Pug

Stuffed Pug

Star light, star bright,
First star I see tonight,
I wish I may, I wish I might,
Have the Pug I saw tonight.

Lovable Pug

Snoring Pug